JOY

FINDS

BONNIE

BY SHARON ROREM

Don't search for joy.

Let it find you.

Sharon Rorem

Bonnie was a very sad little girl. Even though people thought she was a happy girl, she often felt sad inside and she didn't know why.

Her mother tried to cheer her up with new toys, going on trips, and new clothes, but nothing seemed to help.

One day when Bonnie was walking through the park on her way home from school, she had a funny feeling. The feeling was really good and she had never had it before.

GRAMMAR
GRAMMAR
Made
Easy

It lasted all the way home. It was not that the sun was shining, even though it was. Nothing special had happened at school.

She had felt "happy" before but it was not that kind of feeling. It was almost like she was sparkling inside. She was very confused.

She told her mother about it when she got home and they were having their afternoon snack. Her mother said, "Well, that sounds like you found joy!"

Who's Joy?" Bonnie said. "I don't know her." Her mother answered, "Joy is not a person, it's a feeling deep inside that you get when something happens that is good.

Often people look to find joy in different ways." "But I did not look to find joy," said Bonnie. "Joy found me! How did that happen?"

Maybe sometimes it works that way," said her mother. "But I don't understand," said Bonnie. "Nothing changed in my life but I just felt this kind of sparkle inside." "That does sound like joy," said her mother, smiling.

"You know," said Bonnie, "I have so many good things in my life and I have had such sadness inside. I don't know if that sadness will go away forever, but I am going to hold on to this "joy" as long as I can."

"That sounds like
a very good
idea," said
her mother.

That night Bonnie sat
up in bed and thought
a lot about "joy."
She smiled to herself
as she lay there,
finally falling asleep.

From that day on,
Bonnie still had some
sad times, but she
had many more
times where
joy found her.

Life is up and
down, but joy
is waiting
for you just
around the
corner.